I think I have
BUTTERFLIES
in my belly!!

A CHILDREN'S BOOK ABOUT ANXIETY

Diane Sandoval, LCSW

Archway Publishing books may be ordered through booksellers or by contacting:

Archway Publishing
1663 Liberty Drive
Bloomington, IN 47403
www.archwaypublishing.com
844-669-3957

Because of the dynamic nature of the Internet, any web addresses or links contained in this book may have changed since publication and may no longer be valid. The views expressed in this work are solely those of the author and do not necessarily reflect the views of the publisher, and the publisher hereby disclaims any responsibility for them.

Interior Image Credit: Marya Adeel

ISBN: 978-1-6657-3880-4 (sc)
ISBN: 978-1-6657-3881-1 (e)

Print information available on the last page.

Archway Publishing rev. date: 03/01/2023

My name is Titus Jonah Michael Moore.
I love my toys, friends and family galore.
Most days I play and share my stuff,
but one day I realized this wasn't enough.

I noticed something wiggly inside my gut,
it made me feel confused, mad and lots of other stuff.

At school if kids were mean or rude,
it would put me in very bad mood.
I'd get those feels kind of like butterflies...
Butterflies in my belly? I thought I'd cry!!

Teachers saw the tears on my face,
and didn't know how to make it all be erased.
No one could seem to help me calm down,
so I struggled and showed nothing but frowns.

Sometimes at night when the butterflies won,
I felt like I might come completely undone.
My head could not rest on the pillow for long,
because worries had my brain singing the very worst song.
If I could rest my tired head,
bad dreams would wake me right out of bed.

The next day I would not want to go to school, so
I'd tell my mom I couldn't follow their rules.

Other times when my tummy would hurt for no reason at all,
I'd see my friends were just having a ball.
I could've been at a birthday party or a fun time,
but I felt like the butterflies were not doing fine.

When this would happen, I wouldn't know what to say,
if anything, to my parents or that I was feeling this way.

If my parents could tell that something was wrong,
they'd try and they'd try to help me along.
They said that they were very worried about me,
and wanted me to talk with a nice lady.

Mom and dad said she could teach me lots of things,
including how to catch my butterflies and slow down their wings.
I wondered if she had a really big net.
Could it work for me too or would I still be upset?

My butterflies fluttered a lot that day,
when I met with Miss Byrd with whom I would play.
She taught me my butterflies are called anxiety,
and we needed to work hard to set them all free.

She said the butterflies can appear without reason,
they can make me cry and feel like I'm frozen.
I learned that the more I have anxiety inside,
the more I have butterflies even if I don't try.

We drew a picture of my body to color in,
exactly where the butterflies flap, fly and spin.
Miss Byrd taught me that when I'm feeling this way,
I should tell the butterflies that they can't stay.
I can also focus on how to breathe,
which is another quick way to get them to leave.

We made a calm down box to put my tools,
to help me cope and to keep my cool.
Then, we played and played to get my feelings out,
so I could be calm instead of just shout.

Miss Byrd met alone with my mom and dad,
to help them understand why I might seem sad.
She taught them how the butterflies could make me feel,
a little like everything was not really real.

Miss Byrd showed them my calm down box, and
the tools to help me, so I won't feel lost.
She asked them to keep a calm down box at school,
so I can access all my butterfly coping tools.

My parents and teachers are happier now,
because they feel like they can show me how,
to manage my butterflies or other feels,
they know they can be there to help me deal.

Mom and dad are grateful for Miss Byrd for
helping our whole family to be heard.
They like counseling and will take me back,
so I can continue to stay on track.

My name is Titus Jonah Michael Moore
and I know how to continue to explore,
my feelings and the butterflies when they flap.
I can use my coping tools, so I don't feel trapped.

I'm happy to say that I feel calmer now too,
especially since I understand what to do.
I realize my anxiety feels like butterflies flapping around,
and I know I can deal with them in a way that I am proud.

A letter to caregivers; (including warning signs for anxiety).

Dear Parents/Caregivers:

Thank you for taking care of your kiddos by enhancing your knowledge about anxiety. In addition to all that you already do for them, they need you to provide loving and supportive guidance. This is especially true during times your child is experiencing anxiety.

This book is intended to assist with the identification of the symptoms surrounding anxious behavior in children. Some things to watch out for include worries or fears that may or may not be irrational in nature, anger and potential irritability or frustration. As this book indicates, children can also experience a variety of physical symptoms including stomachaches or unexplained body aches. Often, children with more extreme anxiety can struggle to fall asleep or stay asleep, may have nightmares or night terrors and may experience derealization. Additional signs of anxiety in children can include but are not limited to; trouble concentrating, compulsions with order that may present in the placement of toys or items, eating issues, or other behavioral problems such as anger outbursts or acting out. If you notice some of these symptoms in your child and/or have a concern regarding ways to best help them manage their anxiety, please seek professional help. Just remember to bring a butterfly net.

Dedication

I would like to dedicate this book to my children; Kayden, Kennedy, Hudsyn and Henley. May you continue to learn about your emotions and proudly express them with grace.

Printed in the United States
by Baker & Taylor Publisher Services